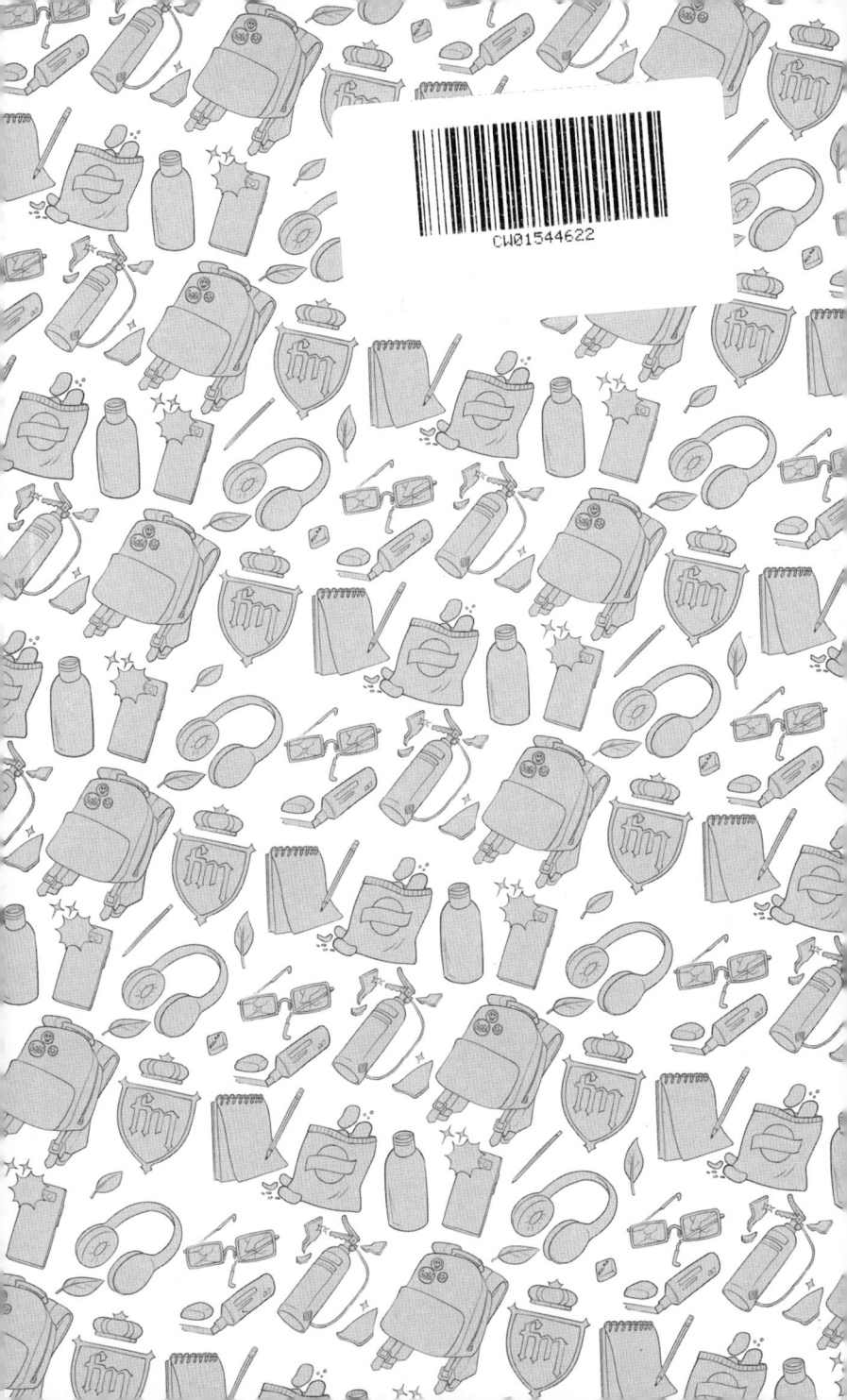

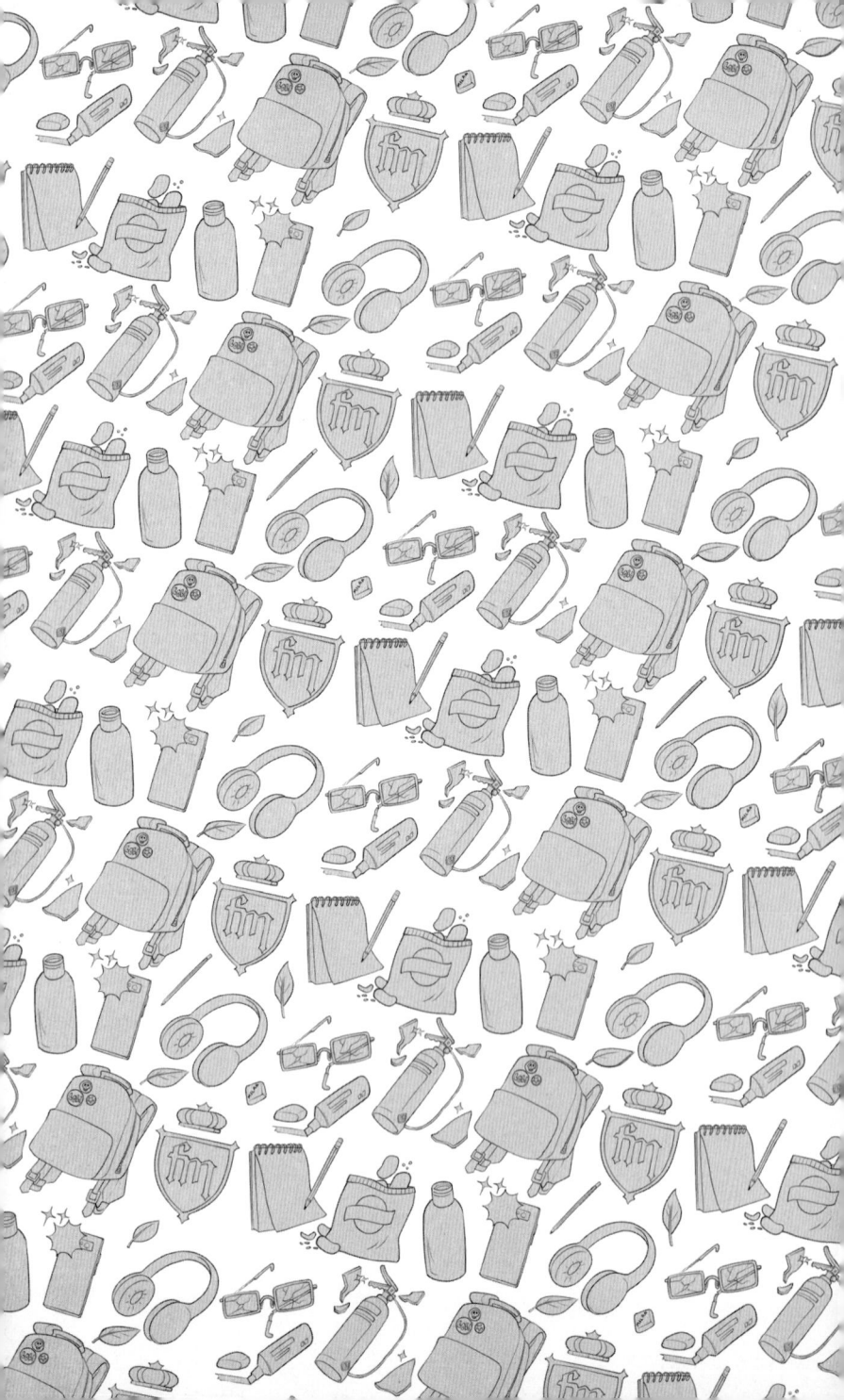

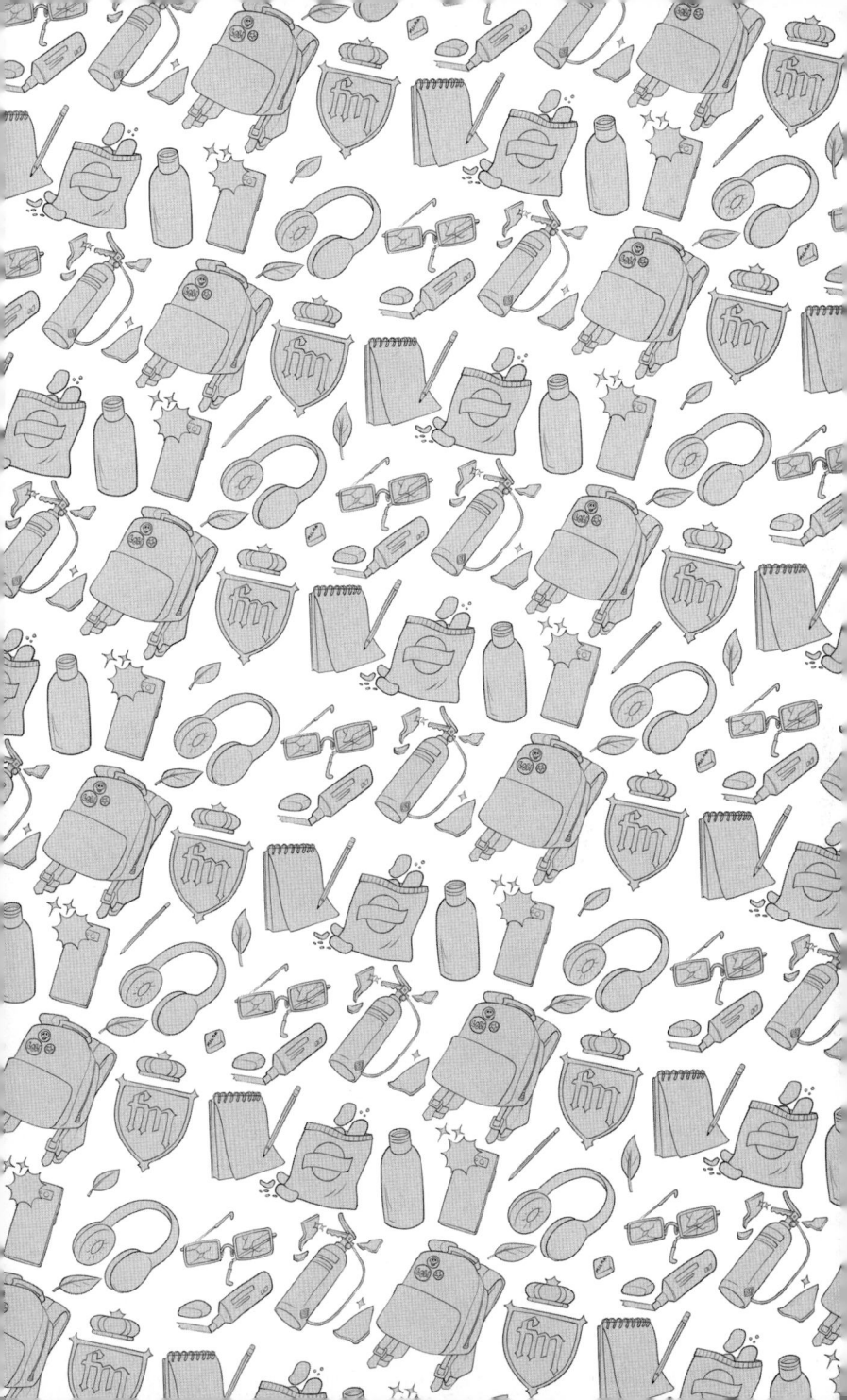

THE
CRASH

THE CRASH

Eve Ainsworth

Illustrated by
Manuel Molvar

Collins

Chapter 1

I just wish I was still with you guys. I hate this dump.

I miss you too Erin, but you'll be OK. I promise.

Erin dropped the phone by the sink and tried to swallow back the sickness she suddenly felt. All of this was wrong.

All of it. She shouldn't be here. The house. Having to share a room with her annoying little sister. This horrible town. This awful school.

She just wanted to be back. Back in London. Back with Jasmine and her other friends. None of this was fair. Text messages weren't enough – she wanted to be with them now.

"Erin! Hurry up! You're going to be late!"

Dad's voice cut through the air. Erin straightened herself up and tried once again to brush her hair, but as always it sprung out into a bush around her face. She opened her mouth so she could inspect her braces one more time, running her tongue over the smooth edges, still hating the feel, and pulled a face. She stared into the bathroom mirror and wondered how she was going to make it through the day.

Fenbrook Manor. Even the name sounded

all wrong. It felt like the school should be some kind of huge, posh building set in beautiful grounds. In reality, it was a crumbling, grey brick building set on the edge of the Ashbrook estate.

Posh and beautiful it was not. And nobody liked her there, not one single person. She wandered the corridors like a sad ghost. The lonely new girl that no one wanted to talk to. She'd been there for months and was still the new girl.

But today would be even worse. Because today she was going on a trip with some of the worst people in her year. The loud, annoying ones. The ones that particularly looked down their noses at her.

The popular ones.

Erin sighed as she turned and left the room. This was probably going to be the worst day of her life.

"You're lucky, I wish I was going on a trip today," Fliss said loudly, pulling a face. "You'll miss double Maths."

Chloe frowned. "It's going to be so dull. A school trip with a load of geeks. I can think of better things to do."

"But Jay Richards is going," Fliss grinned. "That's got to make it more interesting, surely?"

Chloe forced a smile. Everyone in the year liked Jay, but if she was honest, Chloe found him a bit irritating. How could anyone like someone who liked himself more than anyone else.

"You know who else is going?" she hissed. "Him – "

She pointed towards Connor Grant, who was already skulking around the locker area, his dark hair hanging over his eyes. There was a sense of doom and despair that hung over Connor and made Chloe feel uneasy.

"Yeah, well it's not like you'll have to talk to him or anything."

Chloe stared at the note, pinned to the noticeboard, confirming the lucky six who'd been picked as top Art students for a trip to a London gallery to celebrate their talent.

"I don't even know or like any of these people," Chloe scowled. "Who even is Erin Jones?"

"Isn't she that new girl?" Fliss offered. "She's really quiet and shy, but I've heard she's amazing at art."

Chloe's scowl deepened. Well, there was another reason to dislike her even more. "I just hope the day goes quickly. I've more important things to do," she muttered.

"What? Like think about Rae's party this Saturday?"

"Yeah. That."

But as they moved away from the noticeboard, Chloe's thoughts were far from the most talked about party of the year, they were even far away from the school trip and the worry of spending the day with a group of classmates she didn't like.

Because all Chloe could think about was her mother's face when she left the house that morning.

And that her brother had been crying in his room again.

Connor watched as Chloe passed him. He could see the look of disgust she gave him, like he was a bad smell or something that should be avoided, just a rat in her path. He sniffed his armpits covertly, paranoid that he might actually smell. He knew his hair needed a wash. He needed a good night's sleep too.

He pulled his coat tighter across his body and shuffled towards his form room. Maybe this school trip would be a good thing. He might get a chance to grab a nap on the coach, and he would avoid most of the kids that gave him hassle throughout the day.

Except Jay – he wouldn't be able to avoid Jay.

Connor sighed and tried to ignore the dark feeling that overcame him. He just had to hope that today would be a better day.

Chapter 2

Jay was late again, which wasn't great as he had to be on time for the school trip. He wasn't exactly that bothered about going to some stuffy old art gallery, but any excuse to get out of school for the day was good.

He ran pretty much the whole way to school and then slowed up as he approached the gates, making sure he had time to adjust his blazer and smooth his hair down – after all, appearance was everything, Dad had taught him that.

Dad – just thinking of him made Jay's throat tighten. He had to cough and then shake the thought away. He didn't want to worry about it. Not now, not today.

It was supposed to be chilled today.

He spotted the minibus parked in the car park and knew he didn't have long. Quickly, he strode towards the main building and walked over to the school office. Ms Clark always looked after the late register which was good news for him. Ms Clark liked Jay.

She raised an eyebrow as he approached. "The second bell has just gone. This is late even for you, Jay."

He shifted his bag on his shoulder and tried to adopt the sad, sorry-looking expression that always seemed to get him out of trouble.

"I'm so sorry, Miss – it's just my mum isn't well,

and I wanted to make sure she had all she needed before I left the house. My dad isn't home at the moment."

Not the truth, not exactly – but not a real lie either. There were shades of reality there, though. Jay thought of his mum, still in bed with her tear-stained face. He remembered the argument last night, one of many – and Dad's suitcase sitting by the stairs. He didn't like to think of these things.

"Oh no, what's wrong with your mum?" Ms Clark sounded concerned.

"Just a cold, I think. She's struggling to get out of bed." Jay signed his name in the late register and shrugged. "I'm sure she'll be better with rest."

"It's nice you're looking after her, but you'll need to rush or you'll be late for first lesson." Ms Clark paused. "Usually, you'd get a detention for being this late, but I'm sure I can have a word with your Head of Year."

"Thanks, Miss," Jay said, grinning. "I have

my trip today. I don't want to spoil that."

"Oh – you're one of the talented ones. Well done. I'm sure it'll be an exciting day."

"I'm sure it will," Jay chimed back.

In reality, he expected it to be dull and predictable and that he'd be forced to spend time with geeks.

But then again – if anyone could liven up a school trip, Jay knew he could.

Erin wandered out slowly towards the minibus, clutching her bag close to her body. She didn't like meeting new people at the best of times, so this was a nightmare for her. She only recognised half the names on the list – but those that she did recognise were people she wouldn't want to hang around with. Chloe Stephens made her feel especially uncomfortable – she spotted her straight away, talking to another girl in the car park. Chloe was a loud, confident girl with a barking laugh and a mean gaze. Erin had heard her talking about other people behind their backs and none of it had been nice. She seemed like the kind of person that you had to stay on the right side of.

Across from Chloe, Connor Grant stood on his own, fiddling with the toggles on his hoodie. Connor always had a hoodie on, even though it wasn't allowed in school, and his long dark hair always covered his face. He was in Erin's form group, but never seemed to speak to anyone – instead he seemed to hide in the shadows. Grace, who sat next to Erin in their form group, said that he'd always been a bit strange and warned Erin off getting too close to him as his clothes often smelt bad.

Erin walked over to the small group wishing there was one friendly face that she recognised, but she'd only been at the school a few months – most of the people here were still strangers to her. She wished she hadn't submitted that piece of homework to her art teacher, Mrs Richardson. Yes, she'd taken ages on it and was proud – it was a self-portrait, and Erin had used dark colours and mixed in other images to create a blurry, confused image of her face. She thought it represented her well. Mrs Richardson had agreed and told her it was one of the most powerful pieces she'd seen in a long time.

And so she'd ended up on this trip, with other gifted artists. If she was honest, Erin would have preferred to have spent the day in the Art studio. It was peaceful there and no one would give her any hassle.

Mrs Richardson was on the trip, alongside another art teacher, Mr Webber. They called the group over towards the coach, so that they could check off names. Erin followed the group reluctantly.

"It seems like we're waiting for one more," Mr Webber said, frowning. "Has anyone seen – "

At that moment, there was the sound of

pounding footsteps and a loud voice overtook the rest. "I'm here, Sir. Sorry. I was a bit delayed."

Erin turned to see the grinning face of Jay Richards. Great. Her day was going to be even worse now, she was going to be stuck with him. She'd only had one run-in with him and it hadn't been positive. He'd been behind her in the lunch queue and teased her for being posh when he heard her make her order.

"Hello, Erin," he said, nudging her. "Aren't you pleased to see me?"

"Yeah," she muttered, her cheeks blazing red. "Sure I am."

Connor saw the new girl's reaction as Jay approached her. That was interesting. She didn't seem happy to see him. Connor wasn't used to that. Most girls really liked Jay.

What it must be like to be Jay! He had everything: confidence and talent. Connor could feel his body begin to sag. How was that fair? Why did life dish out stuff in such an unequal way?

He shuffled to the back of the line. He already knew no one would want to sit with him.

Chapter 3

Chloe had made sure she'd got herself a seat at the back of the minibus, next to Jay. Although she found him annoying, he was the only person here worth talking to. Jay had already sat down and opened a bag of crisps and was munching them loudly as he stared out of the window. It'd started to rain, and as they made their way out of school, Chloe couldn't help but look up at the dark clouds and feel a sense of foreboding. She wasn't even wearing a coat.

Across from her sat a girl from her year that she'd never spoken to – Saskia. Saskia was really good at athletics, and in most of the top sets at school.

Chloe didn't like to admit it, but she'd always been a bit jealous of her.

On one of the middle seats was Kayden. Chloe didn't know him very well and what she did know wasn't that interesting to her. Kayden was like a maths genius or something and only seemed interested in people that could talk about chess or space. He was on his phone and ignoring everyone.

Erin sat on the seat opposite, also by herself. Chloe scowled in her direction. There was something about the new girl she didn't like. She was too quiet, too smug.

Chloe liked being the main attraction at school; she didn't want any competition.

It was no surprise to Chloe that Connor sat at the front next to Mr Webber. That kid was so strange. Who else would want to sit with him?

Mrs Richardson was driving but she was already grumbling about the bad weather. Chloe decided she wasn't that much of a confident driver.

"Maybe she'll crash," she joked, glancing at Jay. "Add a bit of drama to the day."

Jay stuffed another crisp into his mouth

and frowned. "I don't fancy getting a broken leg today, cheers."

"Well – anything would be more exciting than this." Chloe puffed out a sigh.

"I don't know what your problem is. Anything's better than school."

Jay scrunched up his crisp packet into a tight ball and aimed it at Erin's head. It hit her ear, and she squealed, turning around and rubbing the skin.

"Wasn't me," Jay laughed, holding up his hands. "I'd never do anything as childish as that."

Chloe looked at Jay and scowled. Sometimes she wondered why everyone else liked him.

Jay was bored. The journey itself had been bad enough. Chloe had gone on and on about nothing interesting, and now they were at the museum looking at boring paintings that he also had no interest in. Yeah, it was better than school – but there were other places he could be.

He kept glancing at his phone, hoping there might be a message from his mum. That she might tell him everything was OK now, that Dad was back home, that the arguing had stopped – but, of course, there was nothing.

He walked down the long corridor feeling a heavy cloud descend on him. Outside, the rain lashed against the high windows. To be honest, he'd rather be out there, getting soaked, than be stuck here with everyone else. He liked Art at school. It was kind of relaxing, but he didn't really want to be on the trip. He frowned as he glanced over at the others. They were already walking ahead of him. Saskia and Kayden were the perfect teachers' pets, staring up at a painting and discussing it loudly with Mrs Richardson. Even Chloe seemed genuinely interested in the display, stopping to look at everything. The new girl, Erin, was sitting and making sketches in her book. Jay had peeked earlier and had to admit they were pretty impressive; he was good at Art but he

was nowhere near as talented as Erin. That only made him feel worse.

The only person who seemed as miserable as Jay, was Connor. He was leaning up against the wall, just staring into space, still wearing those headphones of his. Jay wondered how he even got a place on this trip. He never did anything interesting.

"Hey! Cheer up." Chloe approached him, in her usual bright manner, her hair bouncing on her shoulders. Usually, Jay didn't mind Chloe chatting to him, she was loud and funny and, if nothing else, a good distraction, but today her voice was just *too* loud.

"What, like you? Walk around grinning at everything?" he snapped.

He saw Chloe's expression change. Her eyes narrowed and she sucked in a breath. "Whatever's going on with you, there's no need to take it out on me," she hissed. "I thought we were friends."

"We were never friends," he laughed.

Chloe nodded slowly and then turned. "They were right about you," she muttered, as she walked away.

Jay didn't bother to correct her. He knew a lot of people only pretended to like him, but when they thought he couldn't hear, they called him arrogant, stuck-up, aggressive. He didn't mind anyone thinking those things about him.

As long as they didn't know the truth. That he was scared.

Connor sat alone on the way back. He liked it better like that. On the way there, he'd been forced to talk to Mr Webber which had been awkward and annoying. Now he and Erin had switched seats, so he could just listen to his music, close his eyes and drift away.

Today had been OK. He'd quite liked looking at the paintings, even though he'd stood away from everyone else so as not to annoy them. The building had been grand and impressive; it had felt like another world.

It certainly wasn't anything like his life. Just thinking about what awaited him when the minibus got back to school made his stomach twist. He stared out of the window, pressing his nose against the glass. Outside it was dark and misty. It was already late afternoon. A storm was building, and the rain was fierce, almost like it was trying to break in and reach him.

I wish I could just stop this journey here, Connor thought. *I wish I could stop us going back.*

In the driver's seat, he heard Mrs Richardson suddenly shout out.

The bus skidded and there was a terrible sound of screeching brakes. He thought he heard Kayden yelling, but Connor felt strangely calm.

The bus was going too fast. It continued to skid

and was ploughing straight towards the trees on the left-hand side, and then it began to tip and fall.

They were falling. The screams grew louder, alongside the screech of brakes.

And then there was nothing. Only darkness.

Chapter 4

Erin opened her eyes. For a moment or two, she couldn't remember where she was. She could hear the faint sound of moaning, and in her mouth, she could taste something metallic.

Blood.

She blinked, trying to work out where she was and what had happened. She'd been on a trip. She'd been sitting at the front talking to Mr Webber about her latest project and then … and then they'd crashed.

She felt around her. The light wasn't good, but it was clear the bus was wedged between the trees.

She could feel a cut on her leg nearest the

window but it didn't feel too big. Her left ankle throbbed and when she checked her head, it felt sore. But she was OK. She'd survived.

What about everyone else?

Erin looked over at Mr Webber. He was on the seat next to her. She moved gingerly, trying to ignore the flare of pain in her ankle.

"Mr Webber?" she whispered.

His eyes were closed, and she could just make

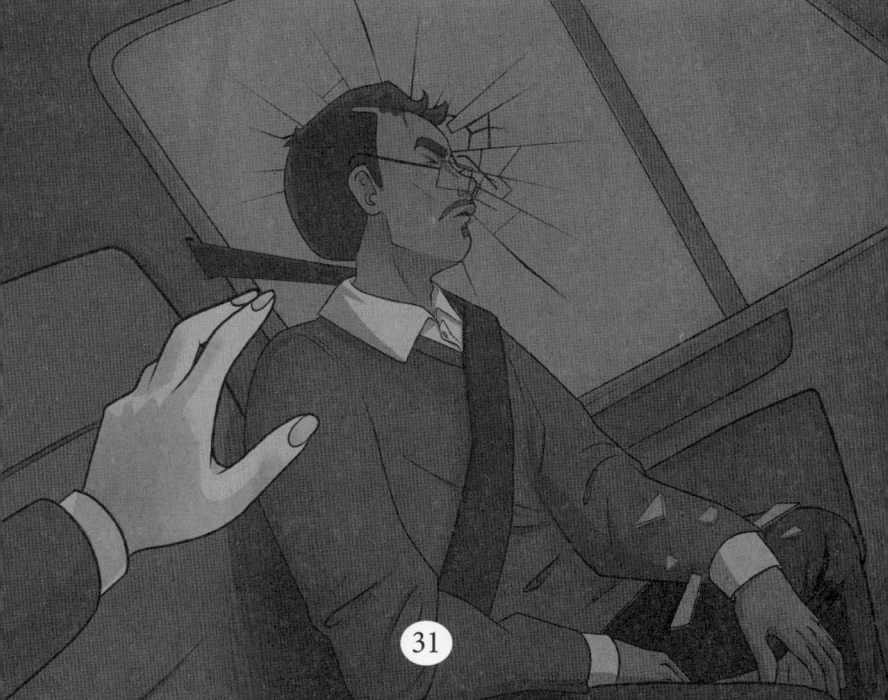

out a pool of blood around his head. That didn't look good. Her heart thudded hard in her chest.

"Help!" she called. "We need help up here."

At first, all she heard were moans in reply. Somebody was sobbing, and then a quiet voice came to her from the back.

"It's OK. We're OK. Hang on."

It was Chloe.

Chloe hadn't been able to move or speak for the first few minutes. She found herself wedged in behind the chair in front of her. Jay was sprawled beside her. Her arm was killing her, and glancing down at it made her feel a bit sick; it was a funny colour. Jay was groaning and trying to move.

"What happened?" she whispered.

"Either we crashed, or this is a really bad dream," Jay replied sourly. "Ow, my leg really hurts. Can you see what's wrong with it?"

Chloe managed to wiggle herself free from her position. Her wrist was still hurting but she gritted her teeth and tried her best to ignore it. She could move it, so she guessed it was only bruised.

"I don't know what happened. Did the bus come off the road?" She peered down at Jay; the light wasn't good, and it was hard to make anything out. "Hang on." She reached in her pocket and pulled out her phone.

Glancing at it, she noticed that there was no signal. It felt like her heart stopped for a moment or two.

"What are you doing?" Jay muttered, groaning again, as he tried to move.

"Hang on," Chloe repeated. She flicked on the torch and shone it down on Jay's legs. His left trouser leg was ripped, and she could see blood, but not loads.

"Can you move?" she asked him.

Jay shifted again. "Yeah, I think so. It really hurts. I think it's my ankle."

Chloe pointed the torch further down. She pulled Jay's sock back, trying to ignore his flinch. She could already see some swelling. "Yeah, it could be a sprain," she said.

But she wasn't a doctor. She knew nothing about stuff like this. Maybe he'd broken it.

Around her, she could hear groans. She shone the torch around trying to work out what was going on. Her breath caught in her throat. It was hard to work out what was where. She could see bags and coats strewn everywhere. On the seat in front of her was Kayden. He was slumped forward in his seat and moaning loudly.

"Hey," she said softly. "Are you OK?"

Stupid question really, but what else could she ask?

"It's my leg," Kayden muttered, not lifting his head. "It's hurting so bad. I think it's crushed."

Chloe tried to use the torch again, but it was hard to see anything; Kayden's body was in the way. She fell back on her heels and rubbed her wrist. It was still throbbing, but maybe shock had overtaken now because it wasn't quite as bad as before.

"We need to get out of here," Jay said. "Who else is conscious?"

Chloe was about to answer when a shaky voice threaded itself across the broken space. "Help! We need help up here!"

Erin. Erin was OK. Chloe felt herself move into action once more. She pulled herself up.

"It's OK. We're OK. Hang on," she called back.

And then, gritting her teeth, she attempted to make her way to the front of the bus.

By dragging his leg, Jay had managed to shift himself up into a seated position. He'd seen the look on Chloe's face when she'd shone the torch down on it – it was clear it wasn't in good shape. He could feel the deep throb in his ankle and waves of sickness that were threatening to overtake him if he moved too quickly.

He closed his eyes briefly and gritted his teeth. All those jokes and banter about crashing, and now look what had happened! He'd give anything to be back on the road, listening to Chloe go on about her latest online videos and how she was no longer friends with certain girls because they'd had an argument.

Jay opened his eyes again and was relieved that the sick feeling had eased. Chloe had moved

to the front of the bus, and he could hear her quietly talking to someone. Kayden was moaning constantly. Jay leant forward and whispered through the gap between the seats.

"Hey, man, it's going to be OK. Help will be here soon."

Because it would be, right? People must have seen them crash off the road. There would be police and ambulances on their way to save them. There might even be a news report about it.

Maybe his dad would see it? Would that be enough to bring him home?

But they'd been on a quiet country road. Jay remembered this because he'd been looking out of the window the whole time. It was dark and stormy outside. Would anyone have seen them come off the road?

The sick feeling was back. Jay sat back again and drew out a long, ragged breath. Suddenly, all he wanted was his dad.

Connor was watching everything happening around him. He'd woken up a few minutes ago but hadn't been able to speak or move. It was as if his entire body was frozen in shock. He watched as Chloe staggered past him. She was holding her arm in a funny way and had some blood on her head. On the seats behind him, Connor could see Saskia was slumped over. She wasn't moving or making any noises. She was either unconscious or …

Connor didn't want to think of the "or". Tears filled his eyes. He had done this. He had caused this. He had wanted to crash and look what had happened.

He wanted to curl up in a tight ball and close his eyes. He wanted to pretend he wasn't here. He didn't want to hear the groaning or look at Saskia behind him.

He wanted to be anywhere but here.

But then someone was shaking his shoulder

urgently. His eyes snapped open.

It was Chloe, except it didn't look like Chloe any more. Her eyes were wide and scared. Her hair was matted against her face.

"Connor, are you injured? Are you OK?"

"I'm – I'm all right, I think – " Connor said, staring down at himself.

"I need your help then," Chloe replied, her voice breaking. "I need you to help me, Connor."

And suddenly Connor felt himself snap into action. He could help make things right again.

Chapter 5

Erin was moving about now. Luckily, her injuries weren't too bad and the shock that had first flooded her body when she woke up had turned into something else, adrenalin. She knew that she needed to check on everyone and try and help those that were injured. She couldn't just sit around waiting for help to arrive. Outside, the rain continued to drum against the bus at a furious pace and the wind howled as if it was in pain too. Erin drew her arms across herself and shivered.

Chloe stood beside her, looking flustered. "Connor's OK. Look – " she said, pointing.

Connor was stumbling towards them.

Apart from a mark on his face, he looked pretty much unharmed. His dark eyes drifted towards Erin, and he nodded awkwardly.

Chloe continued talking, "Jay's awake too, but his ankle is pretty – "

"I'm OK. Honestly."

Erin looked behind Connor and saw that Jay was shuffling towards them. He was wincing in pain with every step, but he seemed OK apart from that. That meant there was four of them. Suddenly, Erin didn't feel quite so alone.

"My leg hurts a bit, but it'll be OK," Jay said quietly. "Kayden's in a lot of pain though."

"He's the one making all the noise," Connor whispered. "Saskia's unconscious too."

Erin glanced around her. Mr Webber looked to have a nasty head injury, but what about Mrs Richardson? Had anyone checked her?

"I'm going to check on Mrs Richardson, see

if she's OK," Erin said, trying to think what was best to do next. "My dad's a nurse so I know some basic first aid. Connor and Jay, can you see how Saskia is? Use your torches, if you can. We need to know if there are any injuries we can deal with immediately."

"What can I do?" Chloe asked.

"Go to Kayden," Erin whispered. "See how bad he is and – I dunno – try and comfort him. Reassure him that we'll be out of here soon."

"But will we?" Jay hissed. He was staring out of one of the windows. "It looks like we're wedged right down a slope, in the middle of trees. Will anyone even know we're here?"

Erin tried to swallow down her panic. "Of course they will. We just have to be patient, that's all."

But her gaze had also fallen on the dark view outside. It looked like the bus was nose down a deep ravine, hidden from view and potentially in danger of slipping further down.

Time was against them.

Chloe was happy to do what she was asked. Usually she hated following instructions, especially from a know-it-all like Erin, but today her mind didn't seem to be working right at all. She was glad someone else was taking charge. She watched as Erin checked on Mrs Richardson, who looked to

be in a bad way. She was sprawled out across the steering wheel and a thin line of blood was running from her forehead.

Chloe switched her attention away from the teacher and moved towards Kayden at the back of the bus; she couldn't afford to panic now. She had to keep herself together.

Kayden was still in the same position, with his head resting on the seat in front of him. Chloe touched his shoulder lightly. Kayden groaned loudly again, making her flinch.

"It's OK, Kayden," she said, trying to stop her voice from shaking. "Help will be here soon. You just have to try and stay calm."

"My leg … My leg – " Kayden gasped.

Chloe reached for her phone again and shone the torch, trying again to look at his leg. The bleeding must be getting much worse because she could see a pool of it building up on the floor beneath him. Her head swirled and she had to bite her lip to keep herself steady.

She remembered that time her brother had fallen and had blood on his face, how long ago had that been? Only a few months. There'd been so much blood, and it had made Chloe shriek from the shock of it. Mum had comforted her and told her it was OK. It was only a nosebleed. Sean would be better soon. It was nothing to worry about.

"Chloe, what are you doing? Why are you just standing there gawking at him?" Jay was behind her.

"I wasn't – I was – " Chloe shook her head, trying to calm herself. "I was just looking."

She gestured with her torch towards Kayden's leg so that Jay could see.

Jay let out a slow breath. "It must've been some of the falling glass that caught you. It looks like it's right in your thigh," he told Kayden.

Thigh? Chloe frowned. She wasn't an expert, but wasn't there a big vein or artery in the thigh? It was one of the few things she'd listened to in Mr Greg's biology lessons.

Kayden groaned again. "I don't feel so good."

"Come on," said Jay, tugging Chloe's sleeve. "We need to speak to Erin. I don't think we've time to sit around and wait."

Jay was pretty scared, although he wasn't going to admit that to anyone. Saskia seemed to be breathing a bit strangely, but he was more worried about Kayden.

He hobbled back up to the front of the bus, with Chloe following in his shadow. He could hear her ragged breathing and knew she was panicking but didn't have time to stop. There was too much other stuff to be dealing with.

"We have to help Kayden," he told Erin, firmly. "We have to stop the bleeding somehow and then we have to find a way to get off this bus. I've checked my phone and there's no signal down here. We need to call for help."

Erin dug her own phone out of her pocket and frowned. "Mine's barely any battery left anyway, and you're right, there's no signal at all."

"Yeah. Well, I wasn't joking, was I?"

Jay looked around him. Some of the windows were smashed, but not totally. He hobbled over to the door, but it was rammed up against a tree – there was no way he was going to be able to open that. He felt panic begin to rise in his chest.

"We can't stay here," he said. "They might never find us. We could be trapped here for who knows how long."

Chloe had flopped down on one of the seats. She looked pale and was breathing far too fast.

"I can't – " she gasped. "I can't – "

Erin crouched down next to her and took her hands. "You can, Chloe. Just breathe with me. Slowly. We can count together."

Jay shook his head. He had no time for this. He shoved past them. "I need to get out of here. I can't stay on this bus a minute longer."

Erin glared at him. "Chloe just needs a few minutes, OK?"

"Chloe isn't the most injured person," Jay said, glancing over at Mrs Richardson and Mr Webber.

He also couldn't get the thought of Kayden out of his head. Connor was still standing near Saskia and didn't seem to be much use at all. But what could they expect from him, really?

"Chloe," he snapped. "You just need to pull yourself together, OK? This isn't all about you!"

Chloe's eyes widened as she stared up at him, but her breathing slowed.

Erin released Chloe's hands and turned to Jay. "So, what do you suggest we do then?" she hissed.

"Well – listening to you isn't getting us very far, is it?" Jay snapped back. "We don't have time. Who made you leader, anyway."

"I never said I was the leader," Erin replied coolly. "I just – "

"I feel sick," Chloe whispered. "Like really, really, sick."

"I don't care," Jay said. "I don't care how you feel, Chloe, because I feel sick too. My ankle hurts, my head hurts, but I'm not going on about it all

the time, am I – "

"Jay!" Erin interrupted. "Leave her alone."

"No – I won't. I need her to – "

"Stop! Stop all of this."

They all turned to face Connor, who'd moved towards them.

"We have to stop arguing. We've got to work together."

It was only now that Jay realised Connor was holding something red. It was gleaming in the gloom.

"Maybe we can use this to smash our way out?" he said calmly.

The fire extinguisher! Connor had found it, rolled under Saskia's seat. He decided that it might be heavy enough to break one of the windows properly.

Connor had spent the last few minutes comforting Saskia as she moved in and out of consciousness. She said her neck hurt, so Connor had taken off his hoodie and padded it around her and told her to try not to move. He didn't know much about this sort of thing, but there was a time when he'd watched a lot of medical dramas on TV to take his mind off the fact that he was alone. It was surprising the things he'd picked up just from that.

Jay was staring at him strangely, like he'd only just seen him for the first time. He took the extinguisher off Connor and nodded slowly. "Yeah," he said softly. "This should work."

Connor noticed that Chloe was looking at him oddly too, but at least she'd stopped that strange breathing thing. Erin was smiling. Connor couldn't remember the last time anyone had smiled at him directly like that before. He quickly looked away.

"Well, I'm not going to mess around," Jay said suddenly. "We need to get out of this bus."

And he walked over to the nearest window and started ramming it with the fire extinguisher.

Chapter 6

Erin watched as Jay banged at the window. It finally gave way after a few goes; she guessed it was already weakened by the crash. Glass splintered everywhere. Jay pulled off his jumper and used it to line the frame.

"I'm going to lean out, see if I can get a signal," he said.

Erin nodded. She still felt numb. Just moments ago, he'd been shouting at her, accusing her of taking over and now he was talking to her again like everything was normal. But how could it be normal? They'd just crashed! Their two teachers were badly hurt. Kayden was apparently in a bad way – and the loudest, most in-your-face girl, was currently crumpled in a seat trying to hold herself together.

Dad had once told Erin that you only see the true side of people when something unexpected happens. Erin eyed the people standing around her, and drew out a breath slowly. She finally understood what he meant by that.

"Chloe, come on," she said, nudging her gently. "We need to help Kayden."

Chloe simply nodded, following her like

a meek puppy.

"What are you going to do?" Connor asked her.

He was still standing there, like a shadow. Erin couldn't work him out at all. She'd never heard him speak before and yet it was him who'd calmed everyone down a moment or so before. Had she underestimated him?

"I'm going to try and think what my dad would do," she told him. "I know a few basics from him; I'm hoping I can help."

Connor nodded. "I'm going to check everyone's bags. Look for food, drinks and more phones. You never know, one might have a better signal."

"Yes, that's a great idea."

At least Connor was making helpful suggestions, unlike Chloe who was just standing there – her face pale. Erin knew that she was panicking but didn't really know what she could say to her to make her feel better. It wasn't like they were good friends!

Erin moved towards Kayden, trying to keep

as calm as she could. She didn't want to make Chloe worse, nor did she want Kayden to realise how bad things were. Because things were pretty bad – Erin realised that as soon as she reached him. Kayden was sweating and his skin was a greyish colour. He'd also stopped moaning loudly and seemed to be drifting in and out of sleep.

"I'm going to try and help," Erin told him gently, trying to sound more confident than she was. She crouched down so she could see his leg better. "I need your phone," she told Chloe. Erin's had now run out of battery, so it was useless. Chloe passed her phone over and Erin turned on the torch and peered down at Kayden's leg. Jay was right; it looked like it'd been cut by some of the shattered glass. The top of his thigh was wet with blood. Erin gently pressed it, and Kayden groaned softly.

"I don't think there's any glass still in there. It's hard to tell."

"I ... pulled something out," Kayden whispered hoarsely. "I thought it would help."

Erin's heart dropped. The piece of glass that Kayden pulled out might have been stemming the flow of blood, but now there was nothing to stop it. She remembered her dad telling her about the major arteries in the body; if these were damaged, you could lose blood quickly. She tried to remember what she needed to do to stop it.

"A torniquet," she said, finally. "I need to make a torniquet."

She looked around, trying to think of what she could use, and then she stared at Chloe. "Chloe, I need your help."

Chloe sniffed. "I'm not sure I can. I – "

Erin softened her voice. "I just need your belt, Chloe, that's all."

"You want my belt?" Chloe blinked at her, confused. "How can that help?"

"It's the only thing I can think of," Erin replied. "I have nothing. I took my blazer off by my seat and I've no idea where it is now. We're running out of time to search for things. Please, Chloe. I need something to tie around Kayden's leg."

Chloe still felt like she was in a dream. She used the nearby seat for support and pulled off her belt. *Maybe I'll wake up soon*, she thought, as she numbly handed it over. *Maybe I'll wake up and this will all have been a bad dream.*

She watched as Erin nimbly wrapped it around Kayden's leg, pulling it tight.

"Isn't that going to hurt him?" Chloe asked.

"It should slow the bleeding down," Erin replied. She hoped that she'd got it right. "Hopefully, Jay's got a signal and we'll be getting some help soon."

Chloe turned away. Looking at Kayden and seeing the blood was making her feel sick. Thoughts flashed through her head of her brother, and she felt herself begin to crumple again. She was always so good at pretending that she was OK, that she didn't need to talk about things – but it suddenly felt like she was being hit with a thousand memories.

"I don't feel so good – " she muttered.

"Well, maybe go and see how Jay's doing," Erin snapped. "I don't have time to look after you as well."

Chloe felt like she'd been slapped. Erin wasn't even looking at her, her face was twisted in concern, and she was sweating as she tried to sort out Kayden. Guilt rushed through Chloe; she knew she should be more helpful, but she couldn't do it – she just couldn't. She glanced down at her hands and realised they were shaking. Kayden groaned again and that was the only motivation she needed to stagger back to Jay.

At least he should have good news. Jay was the sort of person to get things done; he fixed things.

She had confidence that he'd make things better. But as she got to the back of the bus, this confidence slipped away.

Jay was standing away from the window, scowling at the phone in his hand.

"What is it?" she said. "What happened?"

"Even reaching right out of the window – I couldn't get a signal. There's nothing. There's no signal round here," Jay replied sourly.

"There's only one other thing we can do then," a softer voice said. Chloe turned to see Connor staring at them calmly. "Someone needs to get off this bus and find help."

Connor found it funny that they forgot he was there, and when he spoke the others looked at him like he'd appeared out of nowhere. He didn't really care though. He was used to being in the shadows and most of the time he preferred it, after all, no one could bother him there.

But that didn't mean he didn't have good ideas. Connor watched a lot of TV programmes and read a lot of books; he thought about things a lot and he liked to work out problems.

"We need to get off this bus," he said again. "Or at least two of us should. Two of us should remain here and help the injured."

Erin had joined them and was nodding in agreement. "That makes sense. I'm happy to stay here."

"Yes, you should, you're the most useful here because you know a bit about first aid," Connor agreed. "I'll leave the bus as I'm not that injured. Neither is Chloe – she can come with me."

"No, I should go," Jay interrupted. "It's dark out there. We're in the middle of nowhere – "

"You're injured, Jay," Connor pointed out. "You can barely walk. You'll just slow me up."

Jay scowled. "Chloe won't cope out there – "

Chloe stepped forward. Something had shifted in her expression; there was a kind of determination there now. "No," she said. "I want to get off this bus. I need to. I'll go with Connor."

Connor nodded. It was decided. Now they just had to figure out how to get out.

Chapter 7

"You want me to climb through that?"

Chloe stared at the window in horror. Jay's jumper was still covering part of the frame and they'd cleared most of the glass away, but there were still a few spiky bits left. Just the thought of those shards grazing her skin made her stomach clench.

"I'll go first and help you through," Connor said gently. "We'll lay a blazer over the edge. It'll be OK."

Chloe hesitated. The sick feeling was building inside of her again, and she still couldn't feel her legs.

"I can go instead, if you want," Erin said. "You can stay here with Jay, if you think that might be better for you."

Chloe looked around the bus. She could see the two teachers still badly injured. Behind her she knew that Saskia was coming in and out of consciousness, complaining about the pain in her neck, and Kayden – she didn't even want to think about Kayden. That blood on his thigh. The sickness rose in her throat. "No – no, it's fine. I want to get off."

She watched as Connor clambered out first. It was lucky he was so skinny as the space wasn't that big. She heard his grunt as he landed on the other side.

"Are you OK?" Jay called down.

"Yeah – yeah – it's just a bit uneven out here," Connor replied. "Chloe, come out slowly, I'll help you down."

"Just walk as far as you need until you get a signal," Erin said. "Or if that doesn't work, see if you can find the road."

Chloe nodded. She knew what they needed to do.

She sucked in a deep breath and carefully pulled herself through the window. The blazer shifted under her, and she flinched when a sharp piece of glass almost caught her stomach as she pulled herself through. Connor reached up and helped to guide her down. Another piece of glass snagged on her leg, and she yelled out in pain. She fell to the ground next to Connor, tears stinging her eyes.

"I'm sorry – did you get hurt?" Connor asked gently.

"A bit." Chloe touched her leg and flinched. It hurt but it wasn't that bad. She was glad the light wasn't great out here and she couldn't see it.

"I guess we start walking then," Connor replied softly.

Chloe looked around them. The bus looked like it was wedged in some kind of ravine. All around them were trees and undergrowth. She couldn't even hear the road.

"Which way do we go?" she asked.

Connor pointed. Chloe could now make out flattened trees and bushes that formed a kind of track.

"I guess we go the way we came in," he said.

They started walking, pausing every now and then to check their phones. The bus had fallen quite a way, so Chloe guessed that was why the signal was so bad. That and the fact they'd been on a quiet country road.

"Are you OK?" Connor asked her, after a few minutes of walking. "Your leg, I mean. Where you caught it on the glass?"

Chloe touched her leg and flinched again. There was no blood, but it was sore. "Yeah ... I'm OK." She couldn't hide the wobble in her voice.

"Earlier – you looked like you were having a panic attack," Connor continued. "I've not had one before, but they look scary."

Chloe stopped walking and looked towards him, blinking. The light was almost totally fading now, and Connor was becoming a fuzzy outline. It was difficult to remember him as the kid in the hoodie who everyone laughed about. Here, he seemed so kind and calm. He was the only one who knew how horrible she was feeling.

"It's the blood," she admitted, finally. "I hate seeing it. I know that makes me sound weak, but – " She couldn't continue. Tears were building again. She tried to swipe them away.

"It's not weak," Connor said firmly. "Lots of people are like that."

"Yeah, but I should be used to it – " Chloe sucked in a breath and then shook her head slowly. "My older brother, he's really poorly. He has been for some time. He has a tumour in his brain – " She paused for a moment, unsure why she was telling Connor all of this. But it was so calm out here, so peaceful, and Connor was listening, really listening to her. He didn't see loud, confident Chloe – he saw what she was really like.

"He's having treatment, but there are side effects. He has bad seizures. One time, he fell and hit his head. There was so much blood – "

"I'm so sorry, Chloe," Connor said gently.

She shrugged. "It's OK, I thought I was dealing with it. I go out with my friends, I distract myself. But seeing all the blood today, being trapped and feeling hopeless. It just brought it all back."

"Yeah," Connor sighed. "I get that. It must be so hard for you. I'm sorry."

They carried on walking. Connor held his phone up again, but there was still nothing. He strained his eyes – trying to see ahead, but only trees and high bushes were in front of his view.

"You're always sad," Chloe said, suddenly. "You get teased for it all the time. For being on your own. For hiding away. What's really going on with you, Connor?"

He stiffened. "Nothing. Nothing's going on."

Chloe tugged on his arm. "Come on, that's not fair. I told you about my brother and now we're stuck out here together in the freezing dark. Tell me what it is."

Connor spun around. His heart was beating hard in his chest. Why would he tell someone so popular and loud and who lived in a big house with loving parents? She'd never understand. But there was something different about Chloe now. Her expression was softer, her eyes were wide and expressive – not hard and cruel. Something tugged inside Connor. It was a need to tell someone.

"I don't have anywhere to live," he said, finally.

Chloe gasped. "What do you mean, you don't have anywhere to live?"

"Just that," Connor shrugged again. "My mum – she isn't well – she can't cope with having me in the flat any more. So, I kind of stay where I can – my aunt can have me some nights, on her sofa. I can stay at my nan's at the weekend, but that's too far away from school. Sometimes, my friend Toby sneaks me into his house."

Chloe's shocked expression stayed on her face.

Connor pulled a face. "I can't exactly wash my uniform at the moment, and getting showers every day is hard."

"Connor, you can't carry on like this. You need to tell someone. A teacher."

Connor thought of his mum back at her flat. Sometimes, it had been OK, but then she'd get one of her bad moods and everything would change. Despite everything though, he didn't want to get her into trouble.

"Come on," he said instead. "We need to keep walking. We need to get this signal."

And ignoring Chloe's protests, he trudged on.

Chapter 8

"Why are they taking so long?" Jay demanded.

"Stop complaining and check the teachers again," Erin hissed. "We need to keep a close eye on everyone."

Erin was busy checking the bags that Connor had found and gathered near the front seats of the bus. She found some crisps in one and a metal water bottle in another. She took these and made her way towards Saskia and Kayden.

Saskia was awake again, but her face was clammy. Erin handed her the bottle and told her to drink some of it.

"My neck really hurts," Saskia whispered. She took a few sips and then her eyes fluttered shut again as if she was exhausted. Erin guessed the pain was too much.

Erin checked on Kayden. The bleeding on his leg had definitely slowed, but she knew he couldn't stay like this for too long. His skin still felt tacky, and he was drifting in and out of consciousness, so she couldn't get him to drink.

She walked back to the front to join Jay. He was crouched over Mrs Richardson.

"I can't get her to speak," he said, his voice wobbling a bit. "But the bleeding on her head seems to have stopped and the cut doesn't look that deep."

Erin nodded. "That's good. Hopefully she'll be fine. I think Mr Webber will be OK too." She offered Jay some of the drink.

Jay nodded and took a deep slug of the water. He wiped his lips and took a long hard stare at Erin. "You're totally in control, aren't you? I thought you were one of the quiet ones, but when it comes to it – you know what you're doing."

Erin shrugged. "You don't know anything about me."

"How long have you been at our school now?" he asked.

Erin paused before answering. Jay had never shown any interest in her before. He was the loud kid, always joking about, and yet here he was staring at her like she was the most important person in the world.

"You've only been here for what? A month?" Jay continued.

Erin almost laughed. "Make that four."

"Four months. Seriously?"

"Yeah." Her smile slipped. "And it hasn't exactly been easy."

They sat on the seats where Connor had been sitting before the crash. There wasn't much point doing anything else. They had to just wait for the others to get back now and hope they wouldn't be too long.

"I'm sorry you've had a rough time here," Jay said quietly. "Why did you move anyway?"

"My dad got a better nursing job here. We couldn't afford where we were living before, anyway; it was in London and the rent kept going up. When he and my mum split up, things got hard, you know."

"Your parents split up?" Jay sounded surprised.

Erin thought back to that tiny flat that she, her sister and her dad had first lived in, and she had to fight back a shiver. There were times when they barely had enough food in the fridge, just so they could pay the rent. The move was meant to be a fresh start, and even though she knew she'd miss her old friends, she'd been sure she would make new ones.

"Do you still see your mum?" he asked quietly.

Erin shrugged. "Sometimes. She moved away so it's not easy, but we talk on the phone and stuff. It's OK though – me, my sister and my dad are close."

"You must miss your friends, though?"

"Yeah – it's been hard moving here," she said quietly. "I thought it would be easier, but everyone already has their groups. They haven't got time for someone like me."

"I'm sure that's not true," Jay said.

"What would you know?" she snapped back. "You're one of the popular ones. You have everything on a plate."

There was a brief silence between them. Jay shifted on his seat and then he sighed, staring down at his clasped hands. "You know nothing about me."

Jay wanted to shout at her. How dare she make assumptions. Just because she'd had a rough time of things, didn't mean she had to take it out on him.

But then he glanced over at Erin, and saw the fierce look in her eyes. It must be hard coming to a new school, starting again. He wasn't sure he could do that easily.

"I don't have it easy," he said, finally. "My parents constantly fight, like all the time – day and night. Last night my dad left and said he's not coming back, and I believe him."

Erin turned to face him. "Jay, I'm sorry. I shouldn't have – "

He held out his hand. "It's OK. I know how I act. I make out that I'm confident and so sure about everything, but that's just my way of protecting myself. It makes it easier, I guess."

Erin nodded. She got that.

"You know – you'll be OK," she said, finally. "Whatever decisions your parents make, you'll be OK. Just because they don't love each other any more doesn't mean they don't love you."

"Yeah … Yeah, I guess that's true."

A brief silence passed between them.

"I guess we shouldn't make assumptions about people," Jay said, a slight grin forming on his face. "You never quite know what others are going through."

"You can say that again!"

They both looked up and saw Chloe staring back at them through the window. She was smiling weakly and holding up her phone. "We got a signal," she said. "Help is coming."

Erin and Jay helped Connor and Chloe back on the bus. Something had shifted between them all. There was a calmness there, but also some kind of connection between them. They'd got through this together. Erin told Connor and Chloe how everyone was, and Connor told them how he and Chloe had to walk quite some way to get a signal.

"The ambulance and fire rescue won't be long," he said. "We just have to sit and wait now."

Chloe also, despite Connor's weak protests, told the others about his situation. "We have to help him," she said. "He can't carry on living like this."

"I'm fine!" Connor insisted.

Then there was a soft groan from the front of the bus. They all looked around, startled. Mrs Richardson had opened her eyes! She rubbed her head slowly.

Erin ran to her side. "Mrs Richardson – you're awake."

"Yes – yes. I have been, for a little while now. I heard you talking," she whispered. "I'll help you, Connor. I'll help all of you. Once we get off this awful bus."

Chapter 9

Three months later ...

Erin walked to school feeling different now, lighter. She was no longer the new girl. People knew her name, or if they didn't, they knew she was the "girl from the crash" and the one who probably "saved Kayden's life". It meant that people stopped and talked to her now; she no longer felt invisible.

It'd been a strange time. After the crash, her dad had been so worried about her, but he'd also been so proud, asking her to explain over and over again what she'd done. She hadn't expected to get a message from Jay just days later but, pretty soon, the two of them were either talking or messaging

each other all the time. Jay had become a good friend; someone she could talk to easily and who gave her the confidence to believe in herself, and she felt like she'd helped Jay too. She knew he was still struggling, especially now that he knew for sure that his parents were getting divorced – but Erin had encouraged Jay to talk to his parents and they'd told Jay he'd still see his dad regularly and that things might be easier for him now that they weren't arguing all the time.

Erin met Jay by the gates, as she always did now, and they walked in together. Jay was still hobbling a bit from his broken ankle, but he was out of a cast now and hoping to get back to football training soon.

"Are we still on for lunch?" he asked Erin.

"Of course. I wouldn't miss it. It's an important day."

Jay nodded and then smiled. "Yeah. Yeah, it is."

Chloe was waiting for Connor at the end of his road. She felt happy when he showed up. He looked different now. His clothes were clean and fitted him properly, and his hair was cut and tidier around his face. Although he still liked to wear his hoodie, he still looked fresher and happier. Chloe's friends didn't understand why she liked walking into school with him now, but Chloe no longer cared what they thought. At the start, she wanted to just be a friend for Connor, especially when he moved into his first foster home. She figured he'd need a familiar person to support him.

It'd been hard at first. When Mrs Richardson told the school about Connor, social services were called, and Connor was really angry. For a while, he didn't want to talk to anyone, but Chloe wasn't somebody who gave up easily. She'd followed him around school, insisting that he talk to her, and eventually he had. Before long, they'd started arranging to meet before and after school. They would talk about all sorts of things. Chloe found herself talking about her brother and how worried she was about him. Connor never got bored or asked tricky questions, in fact, he really seemed to care.

On the other side, Chloe encouraged him to talk about his life with his mum and some of his worries that he had about that. Connor was still seeing his mum regularly and he hoped one day she'd be well enough to have him home.

They talked about the crash a little bit too.

"Sometimes I blame myself," Connor told her. "I wanted the crash to happen. I think I was so fed up with how my life was, I just needed a big change. I feel bad – I never meant people to get hurt."

Chloe squeezed his hand. "But you didn't cause the crash, and sometimes out of bad things, good stuff happens."

And their friendship was a good thing – of that, she was certain.

As they walked together today, Chloe nudged him gently. "Remember we have to meet the others at lunch today."

Connor nodded. "Yeah," he said quietly. "I won't forget."

At lunchtime, the hall was packed with students. Erin, Jay, Chloe and Connor sat together. Kayden and Saskia sat opposite them. Kayden had only just returned to school after a long break, and Saskia wore a neck brace for a while – but now she was recovered.

The only thing the group still had was their hidden scars; sometimes they talked about them together – the memory of the bus crashing, of waking up, the fear.

But today wasn't about that. Today was a celebration.

The room fell quiet as Mr Hendry – the head teacher – spoke to them all. Next to him stood Mrs Richardson, whose arm was still in a sling, and Mr Webber, who'd totally recovered after a few days in hospital. Mrs Richardson looked at Connor and smiled. Connor managed a weak smile back. He was glad that she was back, and no longer blamed her for what she did. Connor quite liked his foster parents; they were gentle and kind and gave him the space he needed.

Mr Hendry coughed loudly and then began to speak. "Today, we're here to honour those students who showed bravery in the event of an accident," he said proudly. "They helped one another, they worked as a team and, more importantly, they kept calm in a crisis."

Around them, a ripple of applause filled the hall, along with some whoops and cheers. Connor felt himself flush with embarrassment.

"I wish to present them with an award," Mr Hendry continued, clutching a bunch of certificates. "For their bravery and survival skills."

"As long as the award isn't another Art trip, we'll be OK," Connor muttered, without thinking.

The rest of the group looked at him and then, one by one, they burst into laughter.

Connor looked around him and grinned. Suddenly, everything made sense.

Yes, the past few months had been hard, and yes, the crash had been one of the most awful things he'd ever experienced, but Chloe was right. Sometimes, out of the bad, good things happen.

And looking at his new friendships now – Connor realised that he had more than enough good things to keep him going.

They all did.

Book talk questions

How does the coach crash impact the characters?

How do the characters' challenges affect how they behave?

How do the characters' struggles at school shape their response to the crash?

How do you think you'd be able to help if you were on the coach?

What role does teamwork play in helping the group survive and overcome their situation?

How does the crash act as a turning point for the characters?

How does each character grow or change throughout the story?

What does the story teach about friendship and understanding others?

How does the setting add to to the tension of the story?

Which character do you most identify with in the book?

Ask the author

What inspired you to write *The Crash*?

Eve Ainsworth

I love exciting, action-packed books and TV shows and wanted to write something set in a school. I've been on a few school trips myself (as I member of staff) and started to imagine what might happen if a group of mismatched students were involved in a crash that brought them together.

Do you have a favourite illustration in the book?
All the illustrations are fab, but I particularly love the image of the crashed minibus in the trees. It's very eerie and dramatic.

Which character do you most identify with?
I think I most identify with Erin. She is quiet and quite nervous at the beginning, but after the crash she is the one that knows what to do. I'd like to think I would be useful and calm like Erin.

What do you hope that readers get out of this book?
I hope they enjoy the excitement and drama of the book, but also the message that you should never

judge people too soon. Everyone is carrying their own secrets and worries and sometimes it takes a big crisis to realise who your true friends are.

Which part was your favourite to write?
I loved writing the crash scene and immediate aftermath when everyone wonders what has happened.

What sort of skills do you think would be useful for someone in Jay's situation?
Jay needs to learn to stay calm and listen to others. He's used to being in control usually, but in this situation and due to his injury, he can't do as much as he would normally want. It would be useful for Jay to have some first aid skills as well as the ability to stay positive.

What sort of challenges are there in writing a story that takes place in such a small setting?
It can be tricky to make sure that the action is still moving forward and that the pace doesn't drop, but I actually enjoy writing stories set in small settings. It's a fun challenge!

Published by Collins
An imprint of HarperCollins*Publishers*

The News Building
1 London Bridge Street
London SE1 9GF
UK

Macken House
39/40 Mayor Street Upper
Dublin 1
D01 C9W8
Ireland

Text © Eve Ainsworth 2025
Design and illustrations © HarperCollins*Publishers* Limited 2025

10 9 8 7 6 5 4 3 2 1

ISBN 978-0-00-874479-3

All rights reserved. No part of this publication may be reproduced, stored in a retrieval system, or transmitted in any form by any means, electronic, mechanical, photocopying, recording or otherwise, without the prior written permission of the Publisher or a licence permitting restricted copying in the United Kingdom issued by the Copyright Licensing Agency Ltd, 5th Floor, Shackleton House, 4 Battle Bridge Lane, London SE1 2HX.

Without limiting the author's and publisher's exclusive rights, any unauthorised use of this publication to train generative artificial intelligence (AI) technologies is expressly prohibited. HarperCollins also exercise their rights under Article 4(3) of the Digital Single Market Directive 2019/790 and expressly reserve this publication from the text and data mining exception.

British Library Cataloguing-in-Publication Data
A catalogue record for this publication is available from the British Library.

Author: Eve Ainsworth
Illustrator: Manuel Molvar (Advocate Art)
Copy artist: Randall Reis Zacarias (Advocate Art)
Publisher: Laura White
Commissioning editor: Holly Woolnough
Development editor: Zoë Clarke
Product manager: Holly Woolnough
Content editor: Selin Akca
Copyeditor: Sally Byford
Proofreader: Catherine Dakin
Reviewer: Lisa Davis
Cover designer: Sarah Finan
Internal design: 2Hoots Publishing Services Ltd
Typesetter: Jouve India Ltd
Production controller: Katharine Willard

Collins would like to thank the teachers and children at Grange Primary School, Southwark, for being part of the development of Big Cat Read On.

Printed in the UK

MIX
Paper | Supporting responsible forestry
FSC™ C007454
www.fsc.org

This book contains FSC™ certified paper and other controlled sources to ensure responsible forest management.

For more information visit: www.harpercollins.co.uk/green

Made with responsibly sourced paper and vegetable ink

Scan to see how we are reducing our environmental impact.

Get the latest Collins Big Cat news at
collins.co.uk/collinsbigcat

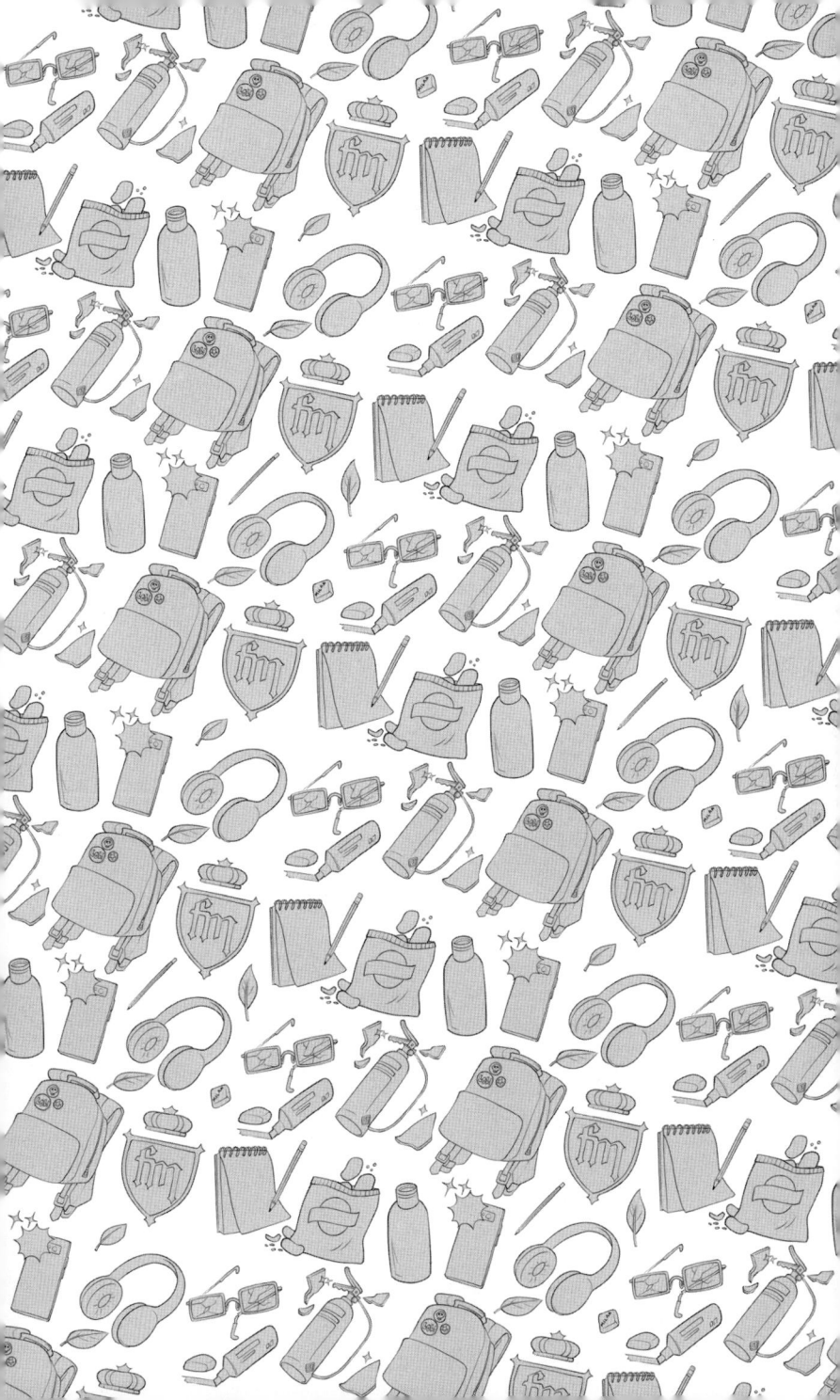

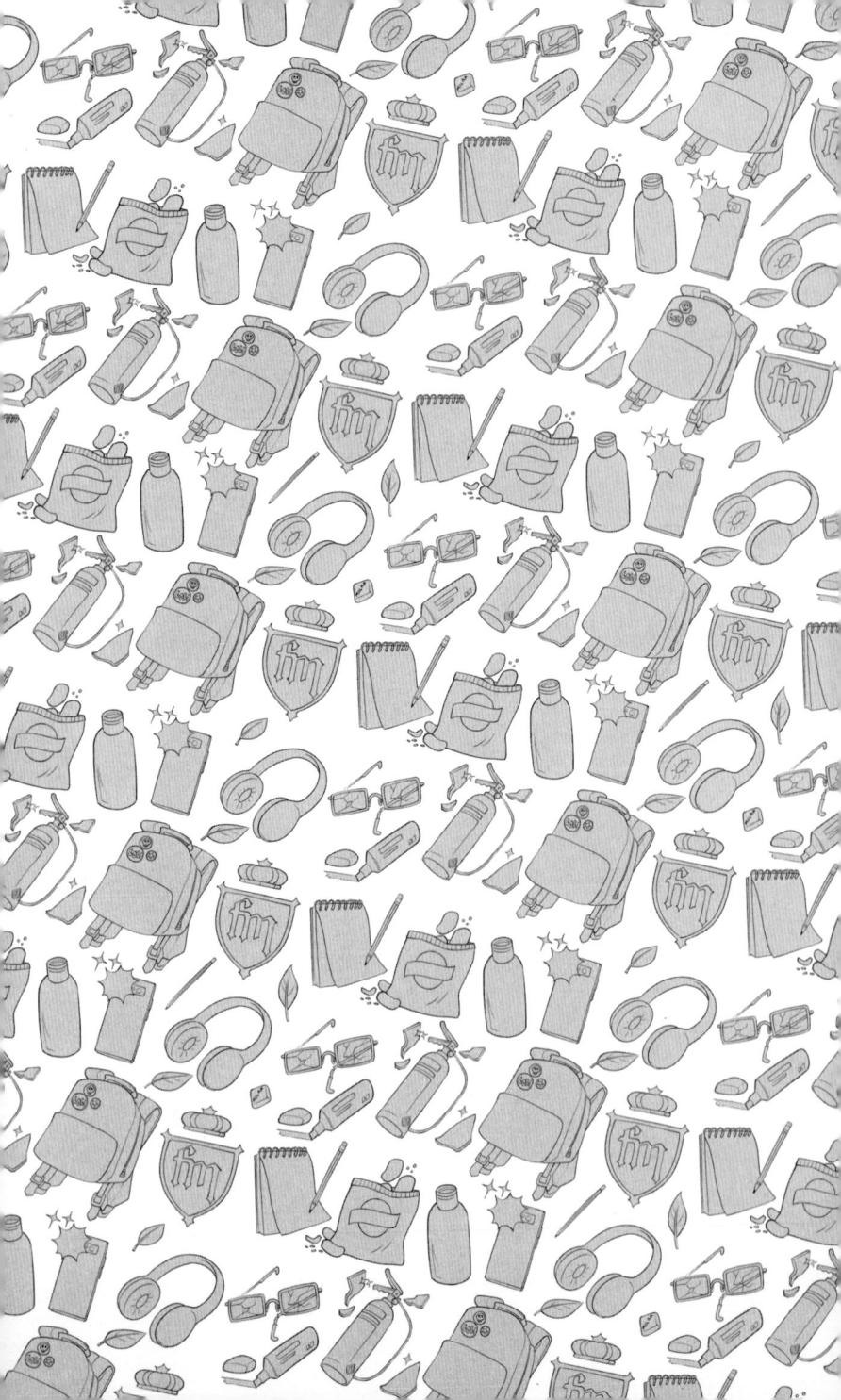